WINGS

Katherine Hengel

SADDLEBACK™
EDUCATIONAL PUBLISHING

DISTRICT ⑬

SADDLEBACK™
EDUCATIONAL PUBLISHING
www.sdlback.com

ISBN-13: 978-1-61651-280-4
ISBN-10: 1-61651-280-6
eBook: 978-1-60291-950-1

Printed in Guangzhou, China
0811/CA21101347

16 15 14 13 12   2 3 4 5 6

1

Angel stood in center field. "One more, boys," he yelled. He pounded his fist into his glove.

He didn't like the lights here. They were too bright. You could lose a ball in the sky. But Angel and the Huskies were up by one. It was the bottom of the seventh inning. They needed one more out to win the game.

Angel knew the batter. He remembered him from last year. Angel never forgot a batter's swing. This guy was pretty good. People said he was slow. That he couldn't meet the fastball. But Angel wasn't so sure about that.

"One more out," he yelled again.

Angel looked over at Roberto. Roberto played right field. The two nodded to each other. "Let's put this one to bed!" Roberto yelled. "Let's bring it in. Right here!"

Angel watched the pitch. The batter was in motion right away. "Here it comes," Angel thought. "He's starting early. He'll meet that fastball. No problem. And probably knock it deep." Angel was ready.

Crack! The ball flew into the night sky. Angel called it right away. "I've got it," he thought. He felt connected to it. He had a way of judging fly balls. Coach Benson said he "had the gift."

He ran toward the fence. He took quick looks over his shoulder. Damn these lights! It was hard to see. His heart raced. But he kept up his pace. The ball was coming down now. Angel could see it clearly again.

His body hit the fence first. Then the ball hit his glove. He caught it! Huskies win! Angel ran toward the dugout. Roberto joined him. "Nice catch, Wings," he said to Angel.

"Thanks, Berto. I lost it for a second! It was a lucky catch."

"That ain't luck, Wings. I've seen you make too many of those," Roberto joked.

After the game, spirits were high. But they had a long ride home. The team walked to the bus. Angel and Roberto were the last ones. They carried their bats and gear. "The sky here," Roberto said. "It's so black."

"Not like the city, eh?" Angel said. "Makes the damn lights seem twice as bright."

Coach Benson stood by the bus. He looked happy. "Great job out there. Both of you," he said. "You're my good guys. I'm glad I get to coach you both next year. Come on. Let's get a move on."

Roberto got on the bus first.

Coach Benson touched Angel's arm. "Angel, wait. I have big news. A scout is coming next week. To the Warriors game. His name's Trent Simon. He's interested."

Angel stared at Coach Benson. He didn't know what to say.

Coach Benson smiled. "You deserve it, Wings. No one deserves it more than you. Come on. Let's head home."

2

Angel walked home in the dark. He felt light and free. Once home, he called his girl, Maria. The phone only rang once. "That was fast," Angel whispered.

"I had the phone by my ear," Maria said. She was half asleep. "Did you win, baby?"

"Yeah. But get this, Maria. A

scout is coming to the Warriors game. Benson said so. "

"Serious?"

"I'm gonna be ready for him too."

"I know you will, baby."

"Go back to sleep now. Sweet dreams, Maria."

Angel hung up the phone. He walked to his sisters' room. The twins were sound asleep. He kissed their foreheads. Then he made his bed on the couch. He always slept there. It was his idea. He wanted Sonya and Cecilia to have their own room. Besides, he was always so tired. He fell asleep in minutes.

Angel heard his mom. It was about 4:30 A.M. "Did you win, *mijo*? My child?" she asked softly. Angel told her about his catch. "*Muy bien*, well done," she said. "I'm off to work. It's Friday. Don't let the girls forget the lunch money."

Angel nodded. "Bye, Mom," he said.

He got his sisters ready for school. It didn't take much. They were seven years old now. Roberto stopped by as usual. Angel and Roberto walked the twins to school. Then they headed to the high school.

3

"Look at this guy, Berto!" Angel said. There was a kid in the parking lot. He was smoking before school. They didn't know who he was. He looked tense.

"That's one nervous new kid," Roberto said. "That one might not make it!"

But Enrique did make it. Central High School was like all the others.

He had been to four in three years. He was a senior. Almost free. The secret was to be a loner. Don't even try to meet people. That was going to be tricky at Central. There was a kid he wanted to meet. Angel "Wings" Hernandez.

Enrique saw Wings play once. The Huskies were down by three. Wings made an inning-ending catch. It was the kind of catch you see on ESPN. Then he crushed one out of the park. Of course, he did it when the bases were loaded.

There was more though. After the game. Enrique saw Wings talk to the pitcher. From the other team! The two shook hands! Enrique never forgot it.

The last bell rang. Enrique had a quick smoke in the lot again. Then he made his way to the field. Roberto and Angel were warming up. Roberto spotted him first. "Here comes the new kid," Roberto said.

"That new kid is a hell of ball player," Coach Benson said. "I put him on the machine. Guy can hit. Says he plays outfield too."

"Is that so? Well, the more the merrier," Roberto joked.

Enrique walked over to them. Coach Benson put his arm around him. "Guys, this is Enrique. He comes to us late in the season. But he's fast. And he's a solid hitter."

Angel put his hand out. "Welcome to the Huskies, Enrique," he said.

Enrique smiled. "I've seen you play, Wings. I'm … uh … I'm a fan, I guess."

After practice Angel went to work. He worked nights at a gas station. It wasn't much money. He couldn't work much during baseball. But every little bit helped.

He grabbed the paper. He scanned the sports section. He blocked out the store music. You had to learn that quick. Or else go nuts.

Angel heard the door chime. Maria came into the store.

"Hey, baby," she said. "How are ya?"

"A lot better now," Angel said. Maria looked good. Even in her work uniform. She still had her name tag on. "How was the diner?" Angel asked.

"The usual. Heaven on earth. Think I should quit now? Since you're gonna be famous once that scout sees you?"

Angel blushed. "That's the plan!"

Maria laughed.

"We're going to get out of here, Maria. No matter what."

"Yeah, me and you. And your mom. The twins too, right?

The door chimed again. It was Roberto.

"Hey, Berto," Angel said. "What up? I thought you had a date tonight."

"Still do," Roberto said. "But I wanted to talk to you."

Maria raised her eyebrows. She took a magazine from the rack. She walked to the back of the store.

"What gives?" Angel said.

"It's this new guy," Roberto said. "He's good, Angel."

"He could be," Angel said. "We'll see. He seems reckless. A wild card. Benson said he changes schools a lot. Must be rough."

"You think he's better than me, Wings?

"Berto, come on. What's gotten into you?"

"Just want to keep my spot. That's all. Coach was right. He's a good hitter. He's good in the field too."

"Enrique just got here, Berto.

State is two weeks away. Who do you think Benson trusts?"

"I'm just nervous, Wings. Want to hit the park this weekend? Hit me some fly balls?"

"You know it, Berto. Of course."

Angel met Roberto at the park that weekend. They spent hours there as kids. Just the two of them. The park was at the edge of the city. It wasn't in a good neighborhood. At all. There were never games there. So it was the best place to practice.

"Looking good out there, Berto!" Angel yelled. "You're gonna upset some Warriors fans on Friday!"

Angel reached down to grab another ball. He saw Enrique by the gate. He couldn't ignore him. "Hey, man," Angel said. "What's up?"

"Hey," Enrique replied. "I heard people in the park. I live nearby. In that white house right there."

Enrique pointed to a complete dump. It was covered in graffiti. It's not like Angel and Berto lived on easy street. But they were a lot better off than Enrique.

"You tired?" Enrique asked Angel. "I've heard you knockin' 'em out there for an hour. Want a break? I can hit some."

Angel hesitated. Roberto probably wanted him to say no. But Angel couldn't turn Enrique away.

"All right," Angel said. He

grabbed his glove. He jogged out to
Roberto.

"I couldn't say no, Berto."

Roberto stared ahead. "I noticed."

4

"I picked the right game," Trent
Simon thought. The parking lot
was full. There were Huskies fans
everywhere. He saw many Warriors
fans too. "Nothing like a high school
rivalry," he thought. "Especially on a
Friday night."

He parked and walked to the
field. He liked to see kids play big
games. That's how you found the

stars. An average player can look amazing on easy days. But not always on the days that matter. This day mattered. At this school. The pressure was on. "We'll see what this Wings kid is made of," Trent thought.

Angel felt good. The temperature was perfect. Nice and hot. He always played well in the heat.

Roberto warmed up with Angel. That's how it always was. But Roberto felt off. He was nervous. He couldn't shake it. He just wasn't right in his mind. Not the way you want to feel before a big game.

Angel saw a stranger talking to Coach Benson. "Berto! You think that's the scout?" Angel asked. "I'll be back in a sec."

He jogged over to Maria. She was standing at the fence. "He's here, Maria. This is it. This is for us. I feel good. I'm ready for him."

Maria kissed him on the cheek. "Good luck, baby," she said. Angel ran back onto the field.

Angel wasn't kidding. He was ready. He was beyond ready. He hit a double in the first inning. It brought two runners in. Then he hit a triple in the third! He owned the Warrior's pitcher now. His bat was hot.

He lit it up in the field too. The Warriors had a runner in scoring position on second base. A good batter was up. Angel had seen him hit it deep. He stood ready. He was up on the balls of his feet.

Angel saw the batter connect. It was a line drive. The ball just cleared the second baseman's reach.

Angel was already sprinting toward it. He dived for the ball. He gave it everything. He rolled out of the dive. He showed the ball. He caught it! His heart was on fire. He knew it was a catch and a half.

"That kid can move," Trent thought. "Unbelievable!"

Maria clasped her hands together. She felt such pride. "He's having the game of his life," she thought.

5

Roberto was not having a good game. He was up first in the next inning. He had two strikes. Then he swung at a ball in the dirt.

Things didn't get any better in the field. There were two outs in the top of the fifth. The Huskies were up a run. The Warriors were batting. A ball was hit in foul territory on the right. Roberto could make that catch in his sleep. But not that night. The ball was in his glove. Then it fell to the green grass.

He dropped it. It took a minute to sink in. What was happening? He heard the crowd's disbelief. The whole city probably did too. Roberto could have ended the inning. Instead, the next batter tied the game.

Enrique sat quietly on the bench. "You gotta catch those," he said. He didn't say it loud. But Coach Benson heard it. And he agreed.

Coach Benson didn't want to lose the game. But he didn't want to pull Berto either. "He'll clean it up," he thought. "He'll keep it together. Wings will step in when needed. Wings will run the field." Roberto didn't make any errors in the sixth. So Coach Benson decided to leave him in.

It was the top of the seventh. The game was still tied. The Warriors' best hitter led off. He connected on the eighth pitch.

It was a hell of a hit to right center. Coach Benson stood up. "Wings will be all over that one," he thought. Angel and Roberto both ran toward the ball. Angel called it. But Roberto didn't back off. Coach Benson said, "Didn't Roberto hear Angel? Back off, Berto. Let Wings take it." He raised his hands to his face. He couldn't watch.

Angel and Roberto both jumped for the ball. Angel had it. He landed

on his left foot. Roberto crashed
into him. Angel's left leg gave out.
Roberto heard it pop.

Angel fell to the ground. He rolled
onto his back. Something was wrong.
He knew it.

"Oh my god, Angel! Did you hear
that? I'm so sorry, Wings. Wings, are
you okay?"

Angel sat up. He showed the ump
that he caught the ball. That was
just the first out of the inning. But it
was the end of the game for Angel.

6

"You tore your ACL," the doctor said. "That's one of the ligaments that holds your knee together."

Angel looked down at his knee. It was swollen and throbbing. He couldn't straighten his left leg.

"What do I do to fix it?" Angel asked.

"You'll need surgery. The sooner

the better. Then a lot of therapy," the doctor said.

Angel sat very still on the table. His mom and Maria stood near him. He heard the doctor's words. Tear. Surgery. Therapy. That would be expensive. Angel tried to focus.

"Say we could. Say we could do those things. Would I … come back? Be the same?"

The doctor took a moment. He chose his words carefully. "A surgeon can tell you more, Angel. Each case is different. It's too early to tell."

Maria drove them home. Angel sat in the front. His mom sat in the back. Silence filled the car. The clicks of the blinker were the only sounds.

"So that was it. My last game," Angel finally said. "The last game of my life. At least I caught the damn ball. I wonder if we won."

Maria looked in the mirror. Angel's mom looked back at her. Neither woman knew what to say. So no one said anything.

Maria drove carefully to Angel's building. Roberto was sitting on the steps. He was still in his uniform.

"Think he's been here the whole time?" Angel's mom said. "It's so late. We were at the hospital for hours."

"At least his knee is in one piece," Angel said.

Maria jumped out of the car. She wanted to open Angel's door. But he moved too quickly. He limped towards the building. Roberto stood up. He wore his worry on his face.

"Angel, I'm so sorry. I lost my head. I was on edge. That was your ball. I ..."

Angel raised his hand to stop him. "Roberto, I cannot do this. Not right now. Not tonight."

Angel limped up the stairs alone. Angel's mom touched Roberto's shoulder. "Berto, why don't you walk Maria home. It's been a long night."

At her house, Maria couldn't help it. She wept for hours. She cried until she fell asleep.

7

The next morning, Angel's sisters woke up early. It was Saturday. They had a lot of questions. Why was Angel sad? What happened to his knee? Angel did his best to explain.

Sonya was confused. "But Berto is your friend," she said. "Why did he do that?"

Angel took a deep breath.

"He didn't mean to. It was … an accident."

He could barely get the sentence out. It was an accident. Wasn't it? It had to be. But why? Why didn't Berto fall back? They had played next to each other for years. Nothing like this had ever happened. Why now?

"Are you mad at Berto?" Cecilia asked.

"No. I mean, I'm mad that it happened. Bad things just happen. I don't know why. They just do."

Maria worked a double shift. After work, she went to the library. Then she went Angel's. She had more than a hundred printed pages.

"Look at these articles, Angel. These are all players who came back. They all tore their ACLs. And they all came back."

She held the papers out to Angel. He was sitting on the couch. He had a stack of pillows under his knee. Keeping it elevated helped the pain.

Angel took the printouts. He dropped them on the floor. "I bet they all had scads of money too," he said.

"Angel, your mom said your insurance would ..."

"It's all over, Maria. Our plan. It's gone. Scouts don't pick guys with bad knees. I'm sorry, okay? It's over."

"But we're not over, Angel. I know a lot was riding on this. But ..."

"Not a lot, Maria. Everything.

Everything was riding on this. Now I'll work at the gas station for the rest of my life."

Maria worked to hold back the tears.

Angel raised his leg off the pillows. He limped across the room.

"What are you doing?" Maria asked.

"I have to call work. They don't know yet. I am supposed to work tonight."

He stumbled to the phone. Maria looked at the printouts on the floor. She couldn't hold the tears anymore. She walked to the door.

"Maria, wait. Don't go. I'm … Mr. Johnson, hi. It's Angel. Listen, I had an accident."

8

Angel woke up on Sunday. He felt horrible. His knee hurt. Maria wouldn't pick up last night. He called her house at least ten times. He hadn't slept. He hadn't showered. He was a wreck.

He could hear the twins in the kitchen. "Girls, you got it in there? Need help?"

"No. We're okay," Sonya said.

Angel looked down at the papers from Maria. He leaned over and grabbed a few pages. He started reading.

He got hooked. He knew most of the guys in the articles. Maria was right. They had all had the surgery. And they all came back. He read each page carefully. Then the door buzzer rang.

Sonya and Cecilia ran to the intercom. It was Coach Benson. "Buzz him in," Angel said.

Coach Benson looked so sad. "How you doing, Wings?"

"Good, good," Angel said. "How did the game end?"

Coach Benson told him. The Warriors scored three runs after

Angel left. The Huskies had one more at bat. But they were too spooked after the accident. They lost the game.

"That's too bad," Angel said. Then there was silence.

"What did the doctor say?" Coach Benson asked.

"It's a tear. My ACL. Doc says I need surgery."

"You gonna do it?"

Angel shrugged his shoulders.

Coach Benson looked down. He took off his hat. "I should have pulled Berto. I almost did, Wings. If I had, then this would not ..."

"It ain't like that. I don't know what got into Berto. But it wasn't your fault."

Coach Benson took a deep breath. "Wings, you're a great player. And you've got a great attitude. You're the best kid I ever coached. You've never had to worry about losing your spot. Berto was worried about that."

"You don't take out a guy's knee. Not just to keep your spot."

"Angel. You know Berto didn't mean it."

Angel looked away. Coach Benson shook his head. "Berto was shook up, Wings. He was trying to show his worth. Earn his keep. That's why he went for that ball. You know that."

"It doesn't matter," Angel said. "It's over. It happened. It doesn't matter why."

"Damn it, Angel!" Coach Benson

said. "Berto just quit the team. He says he can't handle the guilt. You still think he hit you on purpose? To keep his spot? I don't."

Angel's heart sank. He knew Coach Benson was right. Berto loved playing ball. He must be torn up over this.

"The state tournament is next week, Wings. I can't go in short two outfielders. I need you to talk to Berto. He's really beating himself up. He's a good man. So are you."

Angel nodded. "I'll do it. I'll talk to him."

Coach Benson held out his hand. Angel shook it. "One more thing, Wings. You get that surgery. You find a way. And you make it work."

9

Angel grabbed the phone. He stared
at the numbers. He was nervous. He
heard whispering. The girls were
hiding behind the couch.

"Could I get some privacy
please?" Angel asked.

"Call Maria first," Sonya said.

Cecilia disagreed. "No, call Berto.
He's been waiting the longest."

Angel was surprised. "Good idea,"

he said. "Now scram." The girls giggled and ran to their room.

Angel stared at the numbers again. "This is intense," he thought. "Maybe this is how Berto felt? Before the game?" He quickly dialed the number. Of course he knew it by heart. He had been dialing it for years.

"Hey, Berto. It's Angel. Want to walk to school tomorrow? With me and the girls?"

10

There was a home game Monday night. Maria and Angel walked to the field. They walked slowly. Angel worked to hide his limp. His heart raced when he saw the field.

Roberto rushed over. "Did you get it scheduled, Wings? The surgery?"

"Yep. Next week. I'm going to need a lot of fly balls, Berto. It will be like therapy."

Roberto smiled. "I'm glad you're here, Wings. Everyone is."

It was hard for Angel to be there. Coach Benson had Enrique in center field. Roberto was in right. When the game started, Angel teared up. Maria squeezed his hand. Angel squeezed back.

It wasn't much of a game. The Huskies got an early lead. The other team never caught up. Roberto played well. He hit a nice double in the sixth. And he made a hell of a catch in the third. When he did, Angel realized he was smiling. "Nice catch, Berto!" he yelled.

Angel's throat was sore by the end. He even cheered for Enrique. He loved baseball. He couldn't help it. After the game, Angel and Maria tried to sneak away quietly. But Enrique caught up to them in the lot.

"Wings, it's an honor to …"

"You played very well, Enrique. Just stop smoking in the lot, eh?"

Enrique smiled. "No problem, Wings."

Angel and Maria walked home. "I'm proud of you, baby" Maria said.

"We're gonna make this work, Maria. Next season starts in ten months. Doc says I've got six to eight months of therapy. I've got one more chance. We can still do this."

"So can I quit the diner or what?"

"Not just yet," Angel joked.

Angel's mom met them at the

door. Her smile was huge. "Did you win the lottery?" Angel asked.

"Close!" his mom said. She nodded toward the coffee table. There was a letter for Angel. He hopped between the couch and table. The envelope looked official. It was on university letterhead.

"He stopped by about an hour ago, *mijo*. I told him you were at the game. He was impressed."

Angel opened the letter. It was from the scout, Trent Simon. Angel read it out loud.

"Heard about your knee. Tough break, kid. But you'll bounce back. Your kind always does. I'll be watching you next year. Best, Trent Simon."